Frances E. Cooke

An English Hero

The Story of Richard Cobden

Frances E. Cooke

An English Hero
The Story of Richard Cobden

ISBN/EAN: 9783337189556

Printed in Europe, USA, Canada, Australia, Japan

Cover: Foto ©Andreas Hilbeck / pixelio.de

More available books at **www.hansebooks.com**

AN ENGLISH HERO.

A BREAD RIOT.

AN ENGLISH HERO:

THE STORY OF RICHARD COBDEN

WRITTEN FOR YOUNG PEOPLE.

BY

FRANCES E. COOKE,

AUTHOR OF "A BOY'S IDEAL;" "LATIMER'S CANDLE;" "TRUE TO
HIMSELF;" "STORY OF THEODORE PARKER;" ETC.

"All difficulties shall yield to energy."
RICHARD COBDEN.

LONDON:
SWAN SONNENSCHEIN, LE BAS & LOWREY,
PATERNOSTER SQUARE.
1886.

Butler & Tanner,
The Selwood Printing Works,
Frome, and London.

CONTENTS.

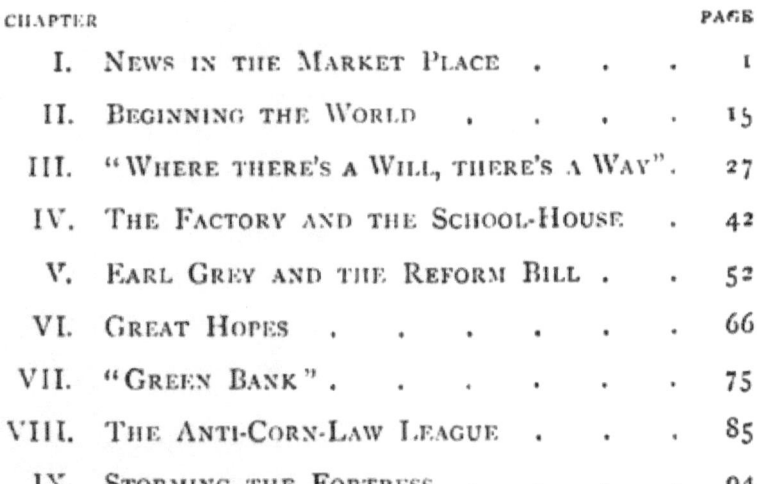

AN ENGLISH HERO.

CHAPTER I.

NEWS IN THE MARKET-PLACE.

In the old Saxon times, a vast forest stretched across the county of Sussex between the chalk hills which form the North and South Downs. In the present day, that district still retains its ancient Saxon name of "Weald," or Forest, though only clumps of trees remain of the once dense wood which covered all the ground.

Eighty years ago, the quiet little village of Midhurst lay in the western corner of the Weald. From the top of a hill close by could be seen, far away to the south, the sparkling waters of the English Channel, dividing our island from the French neighbours with whom we were then continually at war. From the same hill one could look down on the picturesque red roofs of the Midhurst farms and cottages, half hidden by sheltering trees.   Ten miles distant lay Chichester, the chief town of the county, with its old cathedral, its walls, and its four straight streets meeting at the Market Cross.   Country people used to gather near that Cross on market days, and talk over the news from the busy world of which they heard very little all the week in their quiet home life. And truly there was much to hear and tell in those days. · There were tales of victory and defeat of English soldiers in foreign parts, and strange stories of the doings in busy towns in their own land, where the great factories had sprung up, and where men and women in crowded, wretched homes in the midst of plenty had not bread enough to eat.   The state of their own England puzzled the wisest among those country dwellers.   Now and then a better scholar than the rest would mount up beside the Market Cross, on a table in the inn room, and read some startling statement in the latest copy of a paper, which he was fortunate enough to possess.

In those days, the cornfields of America and

the Continent were cut off from England by the war; so every loaf of bread was dear, because English farmers could ask and gain high prices for their grain. Taxes were heavy, too, because of the war. Yet the great, wealthy landowners who sat in Parliament talked of the prosperity of England, while another cry rose from the toiling multitudes who neither owned the land nor sold the wheat. Among the country people of the Sussex Weald, where farmers had been making money by their crops, hard times began to be known. Labourers did not share in their masters' profits, and had to pay dearly for food for the little ones at home. When harvests were bad, few labourers were needed in the fields. Beggars made their way from northern towns with sad tales of want, and people began to long for peace with France, and for news of ships laden with food once more coming into our ports from countries far away.

An old farm-house named Dunford was well known among the homesteads near Midhurst. It had been in the possession of one family for generations, and its door-step was worn with the tread of many feet whose owners had long ago been laid to rest in the quiet churchyard. The house had a red roof and latticed windows, and an old-fashioned garden lay round it. Between Dunford and the neighbouring farms stretched moorland where sheep nibbled the grass in sheltered places, and drowsy bees sipped honey from the flowers all day long in summer.

At the time this story begins, the owner of Dunford was a farmer named Richard Cobden. He was a maltster as well as a farmer, and, moreover, had long been bailiff of Midhurst. There he collected rents and summoned juries, and was well known and respected by all his neighbours. The old farm-house held a large family in those days. Not only did the bailiff himself live there; his married son William and his son's wife, with their little children, found a home with him; and the old man's heart was gladdened by the merry voices and happy ways of the little ones.

On June 3rd, 1804, another grandchild was born, who was called Richard, after his grandfather. The little fellow spent the early years of his childhood safely and happily in the snug house where his ancestors had lived so long. He played about among the sheep and bees during the long summer days, and was warmly sheltered in the snug farm-house kitchen when cold winds blew over the snowy common in winter.

But when the child was five years old, great trouble came to the hitherto peaceful home. Old Richard Cobden died, and the little lad, who scarcely knew what death meant, missed the kind old grandfather, and saw only sad, anxious faces round him. By-and-by the old home was sold, and passed away from the Cobden family. The bailiff had been a good man of business, yet he was able to leave very little money to his son. William Cobden, on the contrary, was a bad manager. He was kind-hearted, and liked by every one who knew him; but he had very little energy, and was, besides, easily cheated. When the old man died his friends shook their heads, and said they feared the good-natured, thriftless son would never make a living for his family.

Just at that time, a little farm named "Guillard's Oak" was standing empty close to the village of Midhurst. There William

Cobden went to live; and he and his wife and children were all glad to stay near the people and scenes they had known all their lives. Mrs. Cobden was a brave, hard-working woman, a good wife, and tender mother. She needed all the hope and courage she had to cheer the spirit of her husband. For, as time passed, the prophecies of his neighbours proved to be true, and the farmers round about him were all more fortunate than he. There is an old saying, "When poverty comes in at the door, love flies out at the window." But this was not true in Farmer Cobden's home. Trouble and ill-luck only bound the little family more closely together. All the children did their best to lighten the father's burdens. Yet life began to wear a sad aspect, even to the young ones. Little Richard Cobden, now no longer the youngest of the family, shared the troubles of his elders. He learned to read and write in the old dame's school in the village, and in his playtime used to watch his father's sheep, spending hours in this business every day, hiding from sudden showers in the sheltered hollows among the trees, and making friends, in the sunshine, of the birds and wild creatures that were his only comrades save the sheep.

Every month affairs grew more hopeless. The eldest boy, Frederick, was sent to America to try to make a living among the many emigrants whom hard times were driving away from England. It was a sad parting; but there was no help for it, for there were many children to feed and clothe. Rent-day began to be dreaded by them all. Perhaps the bailiff who had taken Farmer Cobden's place was not so patient as *he* had been. In course of time "Guillard's Oak" had to be sold. After that the family moved from place to place, till the old happy life they had once led at Dunford seemed like a far-off dream.

Now Mrs. Cobden had a sister married in London, whose husband was in business in Eastcheap, in the city. The bad news of their relatives' ill-fortune reached Mr. and Mrs. Partridge from Sussex. Though times were bad with themselves, of course they must find some way to help. In the end, it was agreed that they should adopt one of the Cobden children, and they chose the little shepherd-boy, Richard. But before he could be of any

use to his uncle in trade, he must learn more
than the village schoolmistress had taught him,
and the boy of ten years of age was sent off to
a cheap school in Yorkshire, where he spent
the next five weary years of his young life.

What a long journey it seemed through the
country that was all new to the little home-bred
lad, as he rode on the top of the coach! How
far away from all his dear ones at home that
dreary school-house seemed! Often and often
Richard longed to be back again at Midhurst,
watching the sheep on the sunny common. He
pined for the kind words that never failed at
home in the worst of times. Ill-taught, ill-fed,
ill-used, time passed very slowly with him in
the Yorkshire school. The distance was so
great, and the cost of the journey too heavy,
for any of his friends to visit him. The only
message he could send home was a letter
written once a quarter by the schoolmaster and
copied by himself, giving a false picture of the
life he really led. The simple, loving family
far away in Sussex read eagerly such letters
from their absent boy, and no one guessed how
wretched his school-days were.

Meanwhile, startling events took place in

England. The gossips in the market-place at Chichester, and in many another country town, had no lack of news to discuss. In 1815, the battle of Waterloo ended the war with France. Then, for the first time for many years, the English were at peace with all the world. Once more all ports were opened. Foreign ships might enter them again, bringing rich freights of corn to make cheap loaves for the hungry multitudes. Men and women in their poor, sad homes, who had borne their troubles patiently so long, took courage, and hoped better times were at hand.

This was true of the towns and the manufacturers of England. But now, when peace was made, the farmers of the Weald and other country places told a different tale. If foreign wheat could be bought cheaply in England, they could no longer get high prices for that which they had grown in their own fields, as they had been able to do in times of scarcity. Good fortune seemed to have left them, and they raised loud complaints.

Now, in Parliament at that time sat great landowners, whose interests were with the farmers, and who knew much less about the

wants of the mechanics and workmen in large
towns. The landowners listened to the farmers' cries, and in that same year, 1815, the
famous Corn Law was passed "to protect home-
grown corn." From that time a heavy duty
was laid on all wheat imported from abroad,
and the result was that the supply soon ceased.
It was a selfish and short-sighted law, and its
ill-effect was soon felt all over the country.
Many looms and furnaces were cold and idle
in consequence ; for foreigners who might not
sell their wheat to us could not afford to buy
the goods we made, and English people had
little money to spend when bread was made so
dear. Hosts of tidy little homes stood empty
now : their owners must emigrate or live on
charity. Poor-rates were high, and work-
houses were full, and a great and bitter cry
rose against those war-and-famine prices in
time of peace.

"Is this a time for patience ?" said the hopeless people. Newspapers were filled with
accounts of mobs and rioting. The gossips in
the market-places of country towns had doleful
tales to tell. Bands of respectable men, bearing
banners with the words " Blood or Bread" upon

them, marched through the city streets vowing vengeance if their hard tales were not heard. In country places the night skies were red with the glow from farms and hayricks set on fire by the bands of wandering desperate men.

In some parts the Riot Act was read. So great was the panic that, at times, troops were called out to disperse harmless people who had met together in some open space merely to discuss their needs. Such a crowd gathered one day in St. Peter's field near Manchester. Sixty thousand persons had left their homes, some of them far away in country villages, and from early morning had marched to their meeting-place in perfect order. This great crowd listened to speeches beneath the hot summer sun, and would have gone home peacefully at night. But, suddenly, the magistrates in alarm sent for soldiers who waited ready for the call; and the helpless people who could not escape in time were cut down by their swords, or trodden under their horses' feet.

No wonder that history tells of the " Massacre of Peterloo," and that the field in Manchester gained a dreadful fame. No wonder that, with such events taking place, the people

of England did not know what the end would
be, or how to mend those evil days.

In the midst of those days, Richard Cobden,
leaving his school life, went to his uncle's warehouse in Eastcheap, London, and began his
work in the world.

PETERLOO.

13

CHAPTER II.

BEGINNING THE WORLD.

SIXTY years ago the traveller by coach from
Yorkshire to London had a long and wearisome
journey. But to Richard Cobden, leaving in
1819 the school where his life had been so
wretched, the way was made bright by hope.
A new life was before him. Who could say
what might happen? When the coach stopped
at last in the city, and stiff and tired he climbed
down from the roof, the dirty streets through
which he went to his uncle's house, and the
little house itself, had a cheerful aspect to him
that they did not *really* wear. Probably his
welcome there was not very warm; for his
uncle and aunt expected little from the son
of the Sussex farmer who had himself failed
in all he undertook. What they did for the

boy was done **somewhat** grudgingly—**not** or
of willing, loving hearts.   **They felt him** as a
burden, and said to each **other** that little good
could come **to** the business from him.

Truly, Richard's early life had been only
a poor preparation.   **Part of it** had been spent
among the sheep **on** the Midhurst Common,
and among the **poor** dame's rough scholars.
He **had** learned very little in the **cheap,** bad
school in Yorkshire **from** which **he had just**
come. This was **all Mr.** and Mrs. Partridge
knew. But something else was true about him.
Deep down within **him lay a** nature that his
wasted, **ill-fed** life had **not crushed.** There lay
a strong love for **his** disappointed father and
mother, **and for the** little country home **where**
life **was so hard.** There, **too,** lay a great
energy, and **a wish to** make **the best** of things,
and to use **well the** small chances that came
in his way.   He **had a** thirst for knowledge :
the little he had learned, **and** learned **so** badly,
made **him** long **to know more.** But all this
his uncle and aunt could not know.   One thing
they *did* discover by-and-by.

When the light of **the** rising sun made its
way through the dirt and smoke of the city

roofs and chimneys into the little garret where he slept, Richard also rose. Then, before the rest of the household were astir, he spent the early morning hours in learning French, and in reading books that he borrowed from a free library in London. " This will never do," said the boy's uncle. For Mr. Partridge could not see that the wiser a man became, the greater his worth might be. Instead of this, he thought that a love for reading was the worst fancy a man in trade could have. So he did all he could from that time to hinder it in Richard.

The boy soon found that he was watched, and his chances to read became fewer. Still, through all difficulties he worked faithfully in his working hours, and he went on gaining all the knowledge he could at other times. Richard Cobden knew nothing about the examples of great men, so he could gain no courage from the thought of the trials and hardships they had gone through. He was just a poor, half-taught lad, who thought his longing to grow wise was the most natural thing in the world, and scarcely knew that before him lay a grand ideal, calling him up-

c

ward and onward—an ideal such as most of
the youths around him knew nothing about.

By-and-by he began to earn a little money
All he spent was entered in a small leather
covered pocket-book, which, dog-eared and
worn, was very dear to him in after years.
They were all small sums he had to spend ; but
this boy, through whose hands so much wealth
flowed in later years, began life with exactness
in little things, and scorned no trifle.   So, in
the leathern pocket-book there were entries of
little gifts to his father and brothers, of odd
pence given to boys poorer than himself, or of
small purchases of second-hand books.

Once in a long while Richard had a holiday.
It was joyfully spent in the shabby little home
at Westmeon, where the family now lived.
On Sundays he was free to do as he liked.
Some miles south of London lies the wide
Surrey heath, where people still love to go and
breathe the fresh country air.   In those days
there was a roadside inn on the heath, where
wanderers could meet their friends and take
food and rest.   The people who kept this inn
became accustomed to the sight of a shabby-
looking, down-cast old man who came on

summer Sundays to meet a dusty, happy-looking youth from London, and spend the day with him on the heath. They saw how the old man went home by coach in the evening, cheered by his holiday; and they watched the youth turn his head again and again to wave a hopeful good-bye ere he set off on his long, weary walk to another week's hard work in the city. These two holiday-makers were old William Cobden and his son. The poor farmer had begun to trust to Richard, and to fancy that some day the broken fortunes of the family might be restored by him. Richard only knew that the holiday cheered his father, and he himself had no greater pleasure than this weekly meeting with the news it gave him from home.

One day, the father and son had a new plan to talk over. An offer had come to Richard which promised well. Far away across the sea, from the quaint old Dutch town Ghent, came a chance for him to go as clerk to some merchants there, who perhaps had seen or heard of him when they did business with his uncle in London. He would have better prospects in Ghent, and there he would escape the many trials which fell to his lot where he was. Richard longed to try his fortune in that foreign town, and told his father of the new offer and his own great hopes. But the old farmer dreaded all changes. He could not look on the plan without many fears, and, above all, he could not bear to part with the son on whom he had begun to lean. In Richard's mind, therefore, there was no longer any doubt. He gave up the new prospects, stayed in London, looked on the bright side of every-thing, and made the best of the few poor chances he had there.

In course of time, Mr. Partridge began to find that his love for books did *not* spoil the young clerk whom he had taken out of charity. He knew that Richard still read French, and studied, when he could, in the early morning hours ; but it was very plain that he did with his might whatever his hand found to do, and that he never wasted a minute of his master's time. Richard Cobden began to be worth a great deal to Messrs. Partridge & Rice (his uncle's firm), and his salary was raised.

Now he had some good news to send to his country home. He had three younger brothers

living there, working for any one who would
hire them in those bad times. These boys
hoped that some day Richard would find something for them to do near himself in London.
They had begun to look up to him as one
much wiser than they were, and whatever he
thought or said had great weight with them.
As for Mrs. Cobden, it is not easy to say how
the remembrance of her good, hard-working
son cheered her. This brave, spirited woman
did not find even her poor, hard life a failure.
Perhaps Richard gained from her his power of
making the most of small chances. However
that might be, Mrs. Cobden found all sorts of
ways of being useful to her poor neighbours at
Westmeon, though she was perhaps the poorest
of them all in this world's goods.

But suddenly the end came. Typhus fever
broke out in the village. As usual, the people
living there turned to her for help and advice.
She nursed a dying child ; and one sad day
she too fell ill and died. Then all their former
troubles seemed light indeed to Farmer Cobden and his children when contrasted with this
great loss.

By that time another member of the family

had settled in London. He, as well as Richard, must learn the mournful news. This was Frederick, the eldest son, who many years before had been sent to the United States to find work. He had fared badly there, and had come back almost as poor as when he went. But there was one friend who welcomed him warmly when he landed as a stranger in the great English city. Richard was heartily glad of his return; and from that time the two brothers, who had been apart for so many years, were great friends. Perhaps the sad news of their mother's death drew them more closely together. They often talked of the future, and made plans for giving rest and comfort to their father in his old age. But in these talks the younger brother always hoped, and the elder doubted. It was plain that if help came from either, it must come from Richard.

In the year 1825, Richard Cobden had been about six years in his uncle's warehouse, and was twenty-one years old. He knew by that time all about the great bales of goods, and the qualities of wool and cotton. It was dull work in the dark, dirty warehouse. Day after day just the same routine. But he put his heart into each little detail of the trade, and forced himself to take an interest in everything. At last the two partners began to think that the energy and talent of their trusty clerk were wasted in this work. Just then they wanted a traveller to visit distant towns and show patterns of their goods, to take orders, and get in their accounts. Who could be better for this purpose than young Richard Cobden ? So they made him traveller for the firm.

What a change in his life! Now he had to spend days in long journeys, among ever-fresh scenes, and to make new acquaintances in each road-side inn where the coach passengers stopped for the night. It was just the kind of life that suited him. He liked well to be able to talk to the strangers in the travellers' room, and to hear about the doings of men, and the wants and events of those stirring times.

This youth, who was only a trader in cotton and wool, would have made a brave knight or a grand reformer in bygone years. But the days of the Reformation lay far away in the past. *Then* the minds of men had been turned towards great struggles for freedom of thought and religion : in late years Englishmen had been fighting battles to gain land in the new world of America, and their thoughts were bent on questions of trade, and on the best ways to find markets for their goods. Such was the field of labour in which Richard Cobden had to work. But the spirit of the worker makes all the difference, and in his common-place calling he became a hero in the end.

Sometimes his business journeys led him to places where grand old ruins told stories of times when men had lived great lives and done great deeds. Then, when the day's work was over, or before the coach left next morning, he used to wander among the broken walls, and enjoy the influence that came down to him from the past. The memory of such quiet old spots went with him on his way through the busy world.

At one time he had to cross the Scottish Border, and he found a new interest in the town of Ayr, where he went to show his patterns, and get orders for the London goods. About half a century before his time, the poet Robert Burns had been a plough-boy in the country near Ayr. Richard was shown the cottage where he had lived, and the places where he had worked and spent so many of his days among the farmers. They were all common-place scenes of every-day life. Yet the imagination that had made Robert Burns a poet had entered into the plough-boy's daily toil, and given a new spirit to it. Just so, though neither he nor any one else knew it, Richard Cobden, carry-ing his bundle of prints, and full of his master's business, was making ready for a grand career never to be forgotten by Eng-lish people.

He went to Ireland, and saw there wretched mud cabins and starving people. The great rivers with no ships upon them, and the towns with no trade, filled him with surprise. He talked to the people, and both there and in England he heard so much of trouble and misrule that he longed to help the miserable people to happy, useful lives.

Often and often tired travellers, sitting round the table in a roadside inn, would forget their dull day's work, **or** weary drive, **as they** listened **to** the talk about the events **of the time,** which **was set on foot** by a travelling clerk from London, **a younger** man **than** most of them. For, above everything, **Richard C**obden began to **care for the interests** of **his** fellow-men, their **welfare and their trou**bles. **He saw so** much **in his travels of the** woes **of the** land, that **he was ready to** discuss **with any one** whom **he met on his way the** best means to bring **about a** better state **of** things.

CHAPTER III.

"WHERE THERE'S A WILL, THERE'S A WAY."

A TRUE story* is told of some seafarers who, once upon a time, formed a new colony in Pitcairn's Island, in the Pacific Ocean. They chose a ruler from among themselves, and for some years all was done according to his will in the island. He fixed the size of each man's plot of land, what plants should be grown, what seeds sown, who should be fishermen, and who should till the ground. No one ever went beyond the shores of the island, or wanted anything that could not be found there.

But, in course of time, children grew up, and the little colony became a large tribe. The

* Used as an illustration in Miss Martineau's "History of the Peace."

people built boats, and sailed to other islands. There they found food they did not grow at home, and changed for it goods they did not want themselves. It is said that their ruler, in his old age, sat before his tent-door on the hill-side, and watched his subjects plying their boats among the neighbouring islands, and was wise enough to see that he must give them freedom, in their changed conditions, to find their markets beyond the borders of their old home.

Now the English people in their larger island were increasing in numbers. They, too, built ships, and went beyond the old boundaries. But at the time when Richard Cobden was traveller for the London firm, the rulers of England were not so wise as that old king in Pitcairn's Island. They wished to confine the English people to the produce of their own island, even if better and cheaper goods were to be had elsewhere. They must live on home-grown corn ; so a bad harvest brought high prices and famine to their doors. The nation was increasing fast. Factories and workshops had been built : yet timber and wool and cotton and silk, if brought from foreign lands, were heavily taxed, that Englishbrown goods might be chiefly used. So it came to pass that many factories stood idle, and English working-men were starving; yet there lay the wide world around our island, with multitudes of living people who had wants of many kinds, and the rulers of England forbade free trade with them.

No wonder that travellers had much to talk about in those days, for England had been at peace for many years, and still there was misery in the land. Yet there were fewer tumults among the people than in the days when the Corn Law of 1815 was passed, for a new and better way of mending matters than that of rioting and bloodshed had been suggested. Of this new way Richard Cobden and his fellow-travellers used to talk earnestly.

In the year 1816 a grey-haired man named William Cobbett, a bookseller in London, had begun to turn his thoughts to the troubles of the people, and to publish a paper, the *Weekly Register*, full of wise counsel on the matter. He was a man who had seen much of life, and learned much from what he had seen. He made sure that the sufferings of the people arose from misrule, and that to give them a voice in Parliament **was the** only cure possible. By **that** means, laws which worked such evil to the country at large might be remedied.

The *Weekly Register* was a cheap paper. It became widely known. Men read it in their **bare**, wretched homes ; or met together in **some** public **place** where those **who** could **not** read themselves listened with eager ears **to** those who could. William Cobbett was not altogether **wise**, but these words of his were of use to the English people. Working-men **turned to** politics instead of to rioting, and spent their energies on **plans to** get a vote, that they might send members to Parliament who *would* make their grievances known there.

In these matters, Richard Cobden took great interest. But he never forgot, **amid** all he had to do and think about, **the** affairs of the little home at Westmeon. **He** wrote often **to** his friends there. **Indeed, the few** comforts they had came from him, and they would have fared very badly without Richard's thought and care. But suddenly, in the year 1826, an event took place which changed all his plans. There was great trouble at Westmeon when his family heard of it. The firm of Messrs. Partridge & Rice failed. They no longer needed a traveller. Richard had no choice. He must take a holiday and go home. He could find nothing to do in London, and no one knew how long this state of things might last.

In that year there were failures on all sides. Banks broke, work was stopped, and a panic spread through the country. At Westmeon, the Cobdens had opened a little shop, with the hope that the villagers, among whom they lived, would give them custom. The troubles in trade spread into that quiet little place. The great London tradesmen, from whom they bought their modest stock, wanted their money just when the poor people of Westmeon could not pay for what they had bought. Into the midst of this trouble came the bad news that Richard, on whom all the hopes of his family were set, had lost his place. It seemed as if every chance of making a living was gone.

But when he came back among them, with his happy way of seeing the sunshine as well as the shadows in life, their hopes rose again. Richard was at hand to consult, and ready to help them with new plans. He even managed

to put some brightness into their lives : for he
would not believe that all was dark and gloomy
because they had some troubles to bear. The
Cobdens had relatives living at Chichester.
One day, he travelled with his sister over the
moors and through the sweet country lanes to
visit them in the old cathedral town. Another
time they rowed across the sunny waters of the
Solent to the Isle of Wight. But before all
with Richard came the wish to relieve and
comfort his father. He soon found that all
new plans must be made by himself. What
was to be done ? Certainly the family must
leave Westmeon. The kind-hearted neighbours would gladly have helped old William
Cobden, but they were all too poor. The
little shop could never be made to pay.
Richard had seen enough of trade to know
that his family must begin business in some
place where people lived who had more wants,
and where life went on more briskly than was
the case in the old-fashioned village of Westmeon.

In the next county of Surrey, among the
great hop-gardens, lay the town and castle of
Farnham. There lived a bishop and his train-

The place was busy with visitors, and the great people helped trade there. It would not be a long way to remove to Farnham from Westmeon, and no better plan offered than for the Cobdens to make a new home there. They felt no pleasure in the scheme, only sadness at leaving the dear old village where they had lived so long. But there was nothing else to be done. By the time the family were settled in the new home, Richard was called to London.

While he had been busy over his father's affairs, his old employers had wound up their business. When this was done, one of the partners entered into trade again. His first act was to send for Richard Cobden, and restore him to his former post of traveller. So the old life began again for him; but very soon a new scheme arose in his mind which he put in action before two years were over. This plan was to begin business for himself, to open a new warehouse in London, and find some Manchester cotton-printers who would send him goods from their mills and give him a commission on all sales made.

Now on some of his former journeys he had

D

met with two youths, who were **travellers** like himself for **a** London firm. He had **found** in them energy, courage, and patience. To them **his** thoughts now **turned.** He told them his plans, and at once they agreed to join him in the work **he** had in view.

It was one **step to have found** willing helpers ; **still** there **were** many difficulties in the **way.** In the first **place,** money would be needed. In the second place, they knew no one in Manchester who would **be** likely to employ them in this **manner.** " Where there's **a will,** there's a way," thought Richard Cobden, **and the** three youths set forth, each by himself, **in search of some one** who would lend them the money **they required.** Richard had not far **to** go, and **was surprised** at his **speedy** success.

In this **time** of **need he thought of** a man whom he had often **called upon in** London when **on his** uncle's business. **This** man had often **spoken** kind words **to the** youth, and praised **him for** his quick, business-like habits. To him **went** Richard Cobden—this time doubtfully **however**—and told his story and his need of friendly **help.** Five hundred pounds were gladly lent. Away went Richard, with a thank ful, happy heart, to tell his comrades the good news. They had had no such good fortune. It was plain that only one share of the sum wanted could be raised. Yet they would not delay; and one morning all three youths took their places on the coach to Manchester to make their next effort, and seek for the willing calico-printer.

What a wild scheme it seemed even to themselves as they talked over their plans on the way. They were filled with hope and doubt by turns. Who was likely to trust three unknown youths? To whom should they venture to apply?

It was the month of September when they made their journey. They were so earnest in talk of plans that they hardly saw the autumn tints on the trees in the country through which they drove, or felt the cold wind which blew round them after sunset. Their first act when they reached the inn was to ask for a list of the chief calico-printers in the town; their second act was to draw lots to decide to whom each of them should go. It fell to Richard's lot to call on Messrs. Fort, who had calico-printing works at Clitheroe, thirty miles away from Manchester,

where the great Lancashire plain rises into
Pendle Hill. He lost no time in setting out
on his journey. Before long, the castle of
Clitheroe, on a hill-top, came in view, and in
due course the doors of the great calico-printing
mill opened in answer to his knock.

He told his errand to one of the owners of
the mill. Mr. Fort listened to his tale, saw
plainly how true and honest the young stranger
was, and took him to his own home for further
talk. As they drove along the hilly road they
were thrown out of the gig. Richard escaped
unhurt, but Mr. Fort was bruised, and blackened
with mud and dust. It was good fortune that
no more harm was done ; but how would he
fare in his mission ? That was the question
Richard kept asking himself, and the answer
soon came, almost to his surprise. Mr. Fort
and his partners agreed to accept, as their
London agents, these three young strangers,
who had concealed nothing, and told all their
poverty and plans. They would trust them
with goods to sell, and wait for full payment.

The fact was, Mr. Fort was a quick judge of
character. He cared less for money in this case
than for honesty and experience and a good

CALICO-PRINTING FROM BLOCKS.

knowledge of the trade. *Now* Richard found out the result of his honest, faithful work during the last ten years. There was no need to pity him that his grandfather and father had both been poor men, and that he was heir to no wealth. Probably if he had not had to help himself and conquer difficulties, he would have been a very different man. His character had grown strong; hope rose high. There was a new field of work before him, and a promise of success in the future.

Richard was chiefly glad of his good fortune for his father's sake. At Farnham, neither the bishop nor the hop-growers brought good fortune to the Cobdens' shop. The old man looked back on his old home with longing. The happiest times in his life were now those when his late neighbours at Westmeon sent for him under the plea that he could help them at harvest time or sheep-shearing. Really, however, the visits were planned to give him pleasure among the old scenes for which he pined so much. On such occasions some kind-hearted farmer would send a horse to meet the old man and help him on his way. For the early part of the journey his children would

walk with him along the country lanes till they
met the escort, and then turn home again
thankful for the gleam of brightness that had
come to cheer their father's lot. Richard
rejoiced that at last there seemed to be a
chance, if his new prospects only proved good,
for him to work for them all and so lessen his
father's cares.

His brother Frederick was still his great
friend in London, and on *his* account there was
one regret in Richard's mind. He would have
been better pleased if this new opening had
fallen to his elder brother's lot instead of to his
own, and he wrote to tell him so in these
words : "I know your heart well enough to
feel that there is still a large portion of it
ever warmly devoted to my interests. I have
not one ambitious view or hope from which
you are separated. I feel Fortune, with her
usual caprice, has turned her face towards the
least deserving. We will correct this mistake
for once. From henceforth, consider yourself
my associate by right in all her favours."

Then the young partners set to work. For
three years goods from Manchester came up
to their London warehouse for sale. Richard

Cobden was glad to think that every day's work brought nearer the time when Frederick should share his fortunes and the dear home circle have a brighter lot.

CHAPTER IV.

THE FACTORY AND THE SCHOOL-HOUSE.

In 1831, before great towns and factories had blackened all Lancashire with their smoke, there lay below the great, lonely Pendle Hill a lovely valley called Ribblesdale. No railway trains rushed through the quiet dale. Travellers drove slowly through the pleasant lanes between high green hedges, sweet with elder and wild rose, or wandered through the meadows by the riverside. They forgot for the time the turmoils of the busy world as they thought of the old days whose memory still hung round Clitheroe Castle or the ruined gates and broken walls of Whalley Abbey. Close to the abbey flowed a clear, broad stream called by the country folks "the Calder," and not far away stood the village of Sabden;

while behind all rose cloud-topped Pendle Hill, with the lonely forest creeping up its slope.

In this quiet corner of the world stood an old factory that belonged to the calico-printers for whom Richard Cobden and his partners were agents in London. It happened that just when the owners of the factory were growing old, and wanted to lead peaceful lives free from the cares of trade, the three young men wished to begin to print their own calicoes. So a compact was made, and the old Sabden Mill changed hands.

It was a strange, sleepy place for a mill full of whirring, noisy wheels to stand in ; the old abbey lying near at hand with the quiet stream flowing past its walls into the meadows ; the great wide moor beyond, inviting for a walk and happy holiday ; and further still old Pendle Hill keeping watch over the beauties of the place.

Into the midst, like the knight into the Enchanted Palace of the Sleeping Beauty, came the youth Richard Cobden full of hope and energy, and set to work. " Send me into Lancashire with nothing, and I will still make a fortune," he wrote to his brother Frederick. " All difficulties *shall* yield to energy. One

has only to bring out **all** the powers **one** has
with spirit.   But it must all come from *within ;*
there is no use in trusting **to** outside helps."
Such were **the** thoughts that filled his mind ;
but his words sounded strangely to Frederick
as he read his brother's letter.   **By** this time he
was a timber merchant at **Barnet**, near London.
Richard had used some **of** his **own** savings to
buy the timber yard, and had placed Frederick
there, hoping that he would put **his** heart into
the trade and prosper.   But Frederick knew
little **about** the energy from within : he *did* trust
to outside helps ; and **when these** ceased, he
failed.

    Another change had taken place, too.   The
Farnham home was broken up, **as** that at Westmeon had been.   **When** this happened it was
settled that old William Cobden should go to
live with his eldest **son at** Barnet.   **There** he
used to amuse himself **with** watching the busy
coaches drive **up** and down the dusty highway
on their journey between London and the
North, and found **in** this poor excitement the
chief interest **of his** life.   Sad letters were all
that Richard ever had from his friends.   Sometimes the young man felt as if the heavy burden

of their hopelessness was more than he could bear in addition to his own anxieties. But his brave heart never gave way, and the strong will conquered all difficulties.

Does it seem matter for regret that Richard Cobden in those days gave his whole energy to calico-printing in his noisy mill, and had no time to give to the sweet country scenes about him ? It is said that all his hopes and longings went out towards Manchester and the great towns where toiling men and women spun the cotton for his prints. Perhaps in those busy days he never turned to look at the cloud-shadows on the hills, or went on to the moors to feel the wind sweeping over them from the great Yorkshire plains beyond. It was from no love of money for its own sake that he gave his life up at that time to his trade. Not as a miser would he ever care to heap up gold. He cared little for it, except so far as it helped him to help other people. Yet he had a yearning to prosper in his work, and there was no limit to his schemes and hopes. What use would he make of fortune if it came to him ? He hardly asked himself the question. He only knew he *must* work. To print calico was his calling at

present ; so he kept to it. He took no holi-
days ; spent his days among the busy machines
and in the Manchester warehouses, and did the
duty which lay nearest to him with all his
powers.

Thanks to the honest, hard-working character
of Richard and his partners, the late owners of
the Sabden Mill had trusted them so far as to
leave some of their own capital in the business.
It was a great help to the young men to have
this money, and another event came about
which served them even more. Calico-printers,
until the year 1831, had to pay a heavy duty
on every yard of calico they printed. That
year the tax was removed. Printed calicoes
could therefore be sold more cheaply, the trade
increased fast, and the factory at Sabden
began to be busy indeed. Before long six
hundred people were at work there. Sabden
village grew into a town.

Old Pendle Hill looked down upon a
changed place. Cottages sprang up on the
once lonely moor. Workmen, who had more
leisure than the young master who paid them
their wages, spent idle hours when the mill was
shut at night. Children followed the example

of their fathers and played about the village road and quarrelled by the side of the stream and round the old abbey gates, because they had nothing to do. There was no school in Sabden, and the truth of the old saying was proved in the little town that "Satan finds some mischief still for idle hands to do."

Was Richard Cobden content to turn that sweet corner of the earth into a place of sin and misery that *he* might become rich? From his heart he pitied those little ones who were growing up so idle and untaught, and a new desire was added to his other hopes—to sweep clean and keep in purity and order the spot where so much of his work lay and his money was made. By-and-by a grey stone building began to rise upon the moor. Wondering children stood near to watch the busy workmen hoist the stones and fix each door and window in its place. Long before the roof was on, the news spread that the building was a school-house. In Sabden there were different opinions on the matter. Some people said that schooling would not do their children any good. Then came a new surprise.

In Manchester it had long been the plan

to have training schools for infants. Richard
Cobden sent there for twenty of those well-
trained little scholars, and the Sabden people
came together eagerly to see his curious show.
They could not but see how different were their
own untaught little ones; and very soon the
young idlers at Sabden were filling the new
school-house on the moor.

One of Richard Cobden's partners, George
Wilson by name, fell in gladly with these new
schemes. The Sabden works were now left
in his care, and Richard went to live in Manchester; but he never lost his interest in the
school, and often went over to Sabden to visit
it. Sometimes he wrote to Mr. Wilson to
cheer him in his work. "There is no knowing
how often good works may multiply," said one
of his letters. "Good examples have more
influence than bad ones; goodness and virtue,
by the very force of example, must go on
increasing, and multiply for ever. There are
many well-meaning people in the world who
are not so useful as they might be from not
knowing how to go to work."

With this idea he went one evening to
Clitheroe, and there made his first public

speech, telling his hearers of the great need for schools in the quickly spreading towns, and for fresh workers in the cause of education. So it was not all bread-winning and money-making with Richard Cobden. By degrees the way opened which led to his being the great helper of his fellow-men, and in every little chance for usefulness he threw as much energy as in any of the grander deeds of later life. . Perhaps he never dreamed in the days of his youth how far the example he set would be followed, nor in how many country places schools would afterwards spring up. It seemed a small thing to collect a few idle children in a school-house on the bleak moor ; but when seed is sown, sun and rain are always sent to help its growth when man has done his best.

Meanwhile, Richard's character ripened quick-ly, and he still thirsted for knowledge as much as he had done when a boy. At odd moments, even when his new business most wanted thought and care, he found time to study, and he wrote to his young brothers to induce them to do so too. Here is an extract from one of his letters :—

"I have a great disposition to know a little

E

Latin, and six months would suffice if I had a few books. Can you trust your perseverance to stick to them ? I think I can. Let me hear from you. I want Henry to take lessons in Spanish this winter."

It was often weary work to be all day in the great smoky town, or the huge warehouse, looking after bales of goods, or writing business letters. Yet when night came he might still be found busy—deep in the history of Europe, or reading some old play, or the speeches of a great English statesman dead and gone. It was a rest for him to turn from the cares of trade and city noises to the pages of some poem ; to read Spenser's " Faery Queen " and the stories of the noble knights who fought in old times against temptations, and made vows of pure and noble lives. Yet he had only been a shepherd-boy on the Sussex Weald; but withal he had had, even in early youth, a grand ideal before him, and he *had never let it fade away.*

By this time he had become more like a father than a brother to his circle of brothers and sisters. Whatever Richard said or wished was law to them. Bad news kept coming from

Barnet, where the timber business was failing. Frederick Cobden did not find that all obstacles would yield to energy. The money Richard lent him was lost; then his health broke down. There was no thought of blame in Richard's mind. It only seemed sad to him that fortune did not smile on all alike. Perhaps he wished he could give more hope and zeal to his brother's despairing character. What he did was to write and ask Frederick to come and share his life in Manchester. " I tell you candidly," he said, " I am sometimes out of spirits, and have need of co-operation, or Heaven knows yet what will become of my fine castles in the air. So you must bring *spirits, spirits, spirits.*"

Frederick went to Manchester, and in course of time Richard placed his father and the rest of the family in a quiet country home, where the old man could end his days in peace, and dream of the long life that lay behind him, spent in the old farm-house at Midhurst or at Westmeon.

CHAPTER V.

THERE was great joy among English people when, in 1830, William IV. came to the throne. He was hailed as the " Patriot King."   Men began to hope that better times were at hand, and **that** the reforms **which** William Cobbett had **taught them** to demand would surely **be** brought to **pass.**

But weeks went, and **no** changes were **made.** Still the old Government was **in power,** with the Duke of Wellington **at its head, and** the complaints of the people turned to bitter cries. **In the** south of England the peasants **who worked in the** field **and on** the farms were starving.   The **corn** law and the duties upon food, which **led** to high profits and rents for the great farmers **and** landlords, made no change in the low wages of the labourers. They might eat grass like the cattle if they did not wish to starve, for *they* could not afford to buy food which was so dear.

So at last it had come to pass that starving men and women *did* eat the weeds and nettles that grew by the wayside. They saw their little children dying around them in their wretched homes. There was terrible trouble in those days in the sweet country places of England. No wonder that the rulers of the land seemed more like enemies than friends to the ignorant people. No wonder that these people in their despair were ready for any desperate deeds. They had only to look across the sunny waters of the English Channel in that summer of 1830 to find examples to such deeds.

The people of France had just then, like the English people, gained a new king. But Charles X. had begun his reign with deeds that were contrary to the laws of the land, and the citizens of Paris rose up in wrath against his unjust rule. The rebellion lasted for three days. Then King Charles fled from the city, and his successor, Louis Philippe, began to reign, with a promise of justice and fair-play to the people.

Across the English Channel came the exiled king, and the tale of justice won by the citizens of Paris was told through all England. Straightway, rough, wild leaders rose up there, calling on the discontented to follow them. Every night the skies were red and glowing with the flames of burning hayricks and barns. Mobs went about breaking machines and doing all the mischief they could. For it was said by the misled, mistaken peasants, that they had only to take affairs into their own hands to gain all that they wanted. And what did they want? The answer is soon given—that the House of Commons should *really* represent the people of England. A wise wish; but their efforts to obtain it were foolish and wrong.

Listen to the story of the English Parliament as it came down from bygone times to those days when the people were crying out for reform. It is really a long story; but all that is needful to know may be told in few words.

Far away in the old Saxon times, when the

district where Richard Cobden was born had
gained its ancient name of Weald,—in those
old days the English Parliament first came into
being. Then all the freemen of thinly-peopled
England were permitted to meet in one great
council to advise and help the king. But as
time passed, and the people multiplied and
spread to distant parts of the land, none but
the rich and great cared to take long journeys
to the meeting-places of the council. By the
time the Normans ruled the land the Common
Council of the nation had shrunk to a meeting
of the greater barons and knights of the shire.
So began our House of Lords; but the great
mass of the people had no voice in the ruling
of the State.

In 1216, Henry III. came to the throne,
and the barons soon grew weary of his weak
and vexing rule. Then uprose Simon de
Montfort, the famous Earl of Leicester, and
led the barons on to claim justice from the
king. This civil war ended in the king's
defeat. The Earl, to strengthen the side he
upheld, summoned a Parliament, and called to
it not only the barons and knights who formed
the House of Lords, but two citizens and

burgesses **from** every city and borough in the
land.   **In** this **way** began our **House of** Commons.

But, as time went on, new changes **came to**
pass.   **Many of** the old boroughs of De Montfort's **time had** decayed **and** left **no** trace of
the once **busy** haunts of **men** but a green
mound **or a** ruined wall.   But **they** belonged
to great landowners, who still **sent** members
to the House **of** Commons **in their name,**
gaining **by this** plan **more** influence for **themselves in** the State.   **Yet** great towns which
had sprung up since **De** Montfort's time had
no right of representation, and so their busy
inhabitants had no vote in the counsels of
the House.   Besides these, were other evils
too numerous to tell.   The complaints of the
people, often made before, and now uttered
anew in the year 1830, were **only** too true;
and there were few faithful voices to uphold
their cause.

What was to be done?   **Now,** if ever, a
leader was needed **who** could be **true** to great
principles, and care nothing for the selfish
motives which guided **so** many statesmen in
those days.

Meanwhile, Richard Cobden was at work with his partners, beginning the new business as agents for Messrs. Fort, in Clitheroe. Yet he was not too busy, as we have seen, to watch the signs of the times, and to see plainly that the troubles of his countrymen called for speedy help. Did it seem poor work to him as time went on, to toil all day among machines and bales of calico, and to open a school for a few neglected children in an obscure corner of the land, when this great reform work was waiting to be done ?

Such a thought never crossed Richard's mind. He threw all his energy into each duty as it came, and now he gladly gave his days up to money-making for the large family dependent on his toil. But all the time he was learning lessons of wisdom and experience, and preparing by degrees for the great public duties that awaited him.

Manchester, where so many of his interests lay, was one of the many towns in busy Lancashire that were then unrepresented in Parliament ; and to the Manchester people the grievance was very great. There, as elsewhere, men were eagerly on the watch for

some wise leader to help them in this time of
need, for some response to their cries from the
House of Commons itself.   In that same year,
1830, their desires were fulfilled.

Nearly seventy years before that date, an
old house called " Fallowden " stood not far
from Alnwich Castle, on the Northumberland
coast.   General Sir Charles Grey lived there,
who had taken part in the long wars against
France; and in course of time, for these
services, had been made an earl by the king.
The family owned much land in Northumberland.   The General's elder brother sat in the
House of Commons, and, like most other great
landowners, was contented with the power he
possessed, and did not see why the people of
England should want any changes made.

Such was the state of affairs when, in 1764,
there were great rejoicings in the old house of
Fallowden.   A little boy was born there who
was named Charles after his father, and was
heir to his father's title and his uncle's land.
The child grew up within sight of the stormy
waves of the North Sea, and loved to hear
them breaking, with a roar like thunder, on the
cliffs not far from his old home.   It was a

free, joyful life that he led among the strong
sea-breezes, watching the sea-gulls flying far
out over the water, and the fishing-boats
tossing among the breakers nearer shore. In
course of time, he went to school at Eton,
then to Cambridge. There were great hopes
fixed on him. He was to keep up the family
name, and as a statesman to follow in his
uncle's footsteps.

Perhaps the influences of his free boyhood
acted on him as he grew older. However
that may be, Charles Grey chose out a course
for himself. When he sat in Parliament,
instead of upholding the landowners' rights,
he took the people's part. Years passed, and
again and again this member for Northumberland took up the question of Parliamentary
Reform, each time without success. Sometimes
he seemed to stand almost alone. Yet he was
always true to his principles, and always patient
and brave. In 1830 he was sixty-six years
old. Some men at that age think their work
in life is done, and they have a right to rest.
Not so Earl Grey. Once again he made ready
for the struggle, and the effort to lead the
riotous, untaught people in a better path.

So, one winter's night, from his place in the
House of Lords, he once more told the sad
tale of the people's discontent, and warned his
hearers that only justice and reform could put
an end to the disturbances in the country.
It was no new thing for him to uphold an
adverse cause. He felt now, as he had often
felt before, that he must speak truths which
few men would like to hear. There was a
great silence through the House to listen to
these words with which he ended his speech :—

"We see the hurricane approaching. We
may trace presages of the storm on the verge
of the horizon. What course ought we to
adopt? We should put our house in order ;
we should secure our door against the tempest.
How ? By securing to ourselves the affection
of our subjects ; by removing grievances ; by
affording redress ; by the adoption of measures
of temperate reform."

Newspapers were dear in those times—
sevenpence a number. But poor men clubbed
together to buy a copy. In the towns they
eagerly read the placards on the walls, and
people who could not spell out a single word
themselves heard the news from their more

fortunate companions, and treasured it in their memories. There was great excitement everywhere while the debate lasted. Wherever there was any distress (and few places were free from it) the corrupt state of Parliament was foremost in every mind. When the reply of the Duke of Wellington to Earl Grey's speech was known, the anger of the people caused a panic in the city of London.

" I shall always feel it my duty to resist all measures of reform :" such was the answer of the Premier. No wonder the people in all parts of the land were roused.

Only a few days, and new hopes arose. The Premier resigned, and Earl Grey, the friend of the people, was asked by the king to take his place and form a new cabinet. Then there was eager watching for the names of the new ministers. Was the day so long looked for really about to dawn ? Truly men hoped so ; yet still the riotous ringleaders led on their excited followers to mischief, and still the night skies were red with the glow of their burning fires.

Earl Grey's Reform Bill was preparing. On March 1, 1831, Lord John Russell read it for the first time in the House of Commons. Meanwhile, hosts of men were ready day and night to march from various parts of England to London to support the king and the new Government. It was well known in the House that these waiting people were ready, like armies, to march forth at the first word of command. Their cry was, " The bill, the whole bill, and nothing but the bill." And thus the country waited, and hope changed to fear, and fear again to hope, and a new election took place ; and still, through the long, hot summer days, the House sat on, and the fierce debate lasted through the weary nights.

At length, one September evening, 1831, crowds gathered in Parliament Square, and filled the Strand and all the neighbouring streets. That night, children were startled from their sleep by ringing cheers that ran along the streets and died away and woke again. Before the sun rose, the news that the bill had passed the Commons was carried into the country. Bells were rung and there was shouting and music, and the glad tidings were told even in the villages among the hills.

Then came the question, " What will the

Lords do ?"   Men had not long to wait for the reply.   Earl Grey opened the debate in the Upper House.   It is said that even those who were most opposed to him were touched by his patience and the earnestness with which he spoke.

It would be a long tale to tell in full how the Lords threw out the bill; how petitions and deputations besieged Earl Grey, and how his strength nearly failed in the fierce troubles that followed.   The great riots in Bristol, Nottingham, and Derby are matters of history now.   We read a more welcome story when we turn to the wiser and more patient thousands who gathered from far and near, till a great hill-side near Birmingham was covered with men all eager in one great cause.   By that time, a new Reform Bill was before the Lords ; and one day, while the debate went on among them, 100,000 voices on New Hall Hill were singing the union hymn which every one in those days knew by heart :—

> " Lo, we answer, see we come,
>   Quick at Freedom's holy call ;
> We come ! we come ! we come ! we come !
>   To do the glorious work of all.

And hark! we raise from sea to sea
   The sacred watchword, Liberty.

God is our Guide : from field, from **wave,**
   From plough, from anvil, and from loom,
We come our country's rights to save,
   And speak a tyrant faction's doom.
And hark ! we raise from sea to sea
   The sacred watchword, Liberty.

God is our Guide —no swords **we** draw,
   We kindle not war's battle fires ;
By union, justice, truth and law,
   We **claim the** birthright of our sires.
We raise **the** watchword Liberty,
   We will, we will, **we** will be free."

Against *such* gatherings there could be **no**
need **of** the soldiers **who were** kept ready
armed **to** quell the rebellion which **it was**
feared might break forth.   Though resolute,
they were always orderly and peaceful.   When,
bareheaded, these men vowed **to** devote themselves, through trial and privation, to their
country's cause ; they wished to do **so** by
none but lawful means.   Surely Earl Grey was
fighting **in a** better **cause than that** for which
his father **won** title and honour from the king.

At length, **on June** 7th, 1832, the grey-
haired leader won the love and gratitude of the

people. The Reform Bill passed the House of Lords, and gained the royal assent. From that time, every £10 householder had a vote; the so-called rotten boroughs were abolished, and the great towns, which were the homes of working-men, could at last send messengers to Parliament to tell about their woes.

Not much more work lay before Earl Grey. He found peace and rest in his happy home, whence he still watched the progress of the people. Other leaders must rise up to take his place. One of these future leaders, Richard Cobden, was patiently preparing for the work.

CHAPTER VI.

ONCE upon a time—so says an old story—there lived a fairy who turned everything he touched into gold. No such cunning sprite came to help Richard Cobden in his search for wealth; he must trust to his own energy and perseverance. Yet his partners were surprised to find how their trade increased through his efforts, and what a talent for business he possessed. The calicoes they printed were in great demand; they were making money fast. If matters went on as they were doing at that time, they would all be wealthy men before long. Yet for all that they knew their trade might be much larger than it was. If there were only free trade between England and other nations, their calicoes might be liked and bought in foreign lands.

Far away from the busy lives of workers in Manchester, Richard's old father was ending his days in a quiet country village in Hampshire. Often, amid his day's toil, the young man's thoughts used to turn to this little home, where his sisters also lived. He knew that it would never do to bring the old man among the noises of the town. The best thing to be done was to surround him with sights and sounds that should bring back to him in old age, as nearly as possible, the happy days spent in the Midhurst Farm, where his ancestors had lived. And so, at the end of his life, early, happy memories came round William Cobden, and all the cares and vexations he had passed through seemed to fade away from his mind. But the greatest pleasure he had was to see or hear from Richard, and his last days were brightened by hope for his son's future.

In June, 1833, the old man died. Then Richard took his sisters back with him to Manchester, and they lived together in a large house which he bought in Quay Street. He looked forward to gathering the whole family under his own roof in course of time. Fresh patterns were needed for the Sabden printing works that summer. Richard, glad of the change of scene, went over to Paris to seek for them. His love of travelling was as strong as it had been when he was a clerk in his uncle's firm; and he believed still, as he had always done, that wisdom and experience could be gained from learning the thoughts of strangers. So he took a longer holiday after his work was done in Paris, and for the first time went to Switzerland. The grand lakes, with their guardian mountains covered with snow and lost in clouds, were glorious sights to him, tired as he was with anxiety and overwork. He wandered over the rugged passes and through the sheltered valleys, and talked to the peasants in the villages where he rested for the night. Wherever he went, he found prosperous, happy people, busy over the kind of work that suited both the place they lived in and their own powers. The troubles of the English people often came to his mind in this journey; for he saw the Swiss contented and well to do on their farms; and he found no excise men in that happy land extorting duties that were supposed at home to protect special trades, but really had the effect of injuring all. There was free trade in Switzerland, and he saw clearly by this time what it might do for his own native land. With such thoughts, he came back to England, and took up his work in Manchester again.

Many years before this time, when only a boy with plenty of ready wit, but without much thoughtful wisdom, Richard wrote a play called " The Phrenologist." He spent much time in preparing it, and it would not be easy to tell what great hopes filled his mind when he looked at it for the last time, folded it up, and sent it to the manager of a London theatre. Days passed, and he heard nothing of its fate. Meanwhile, he built grand castles in the air. His play would surely be acted on the stage, and become famous. When suddenly, down came his airy castles, and all his hopes fell. The manager of the theatre declined his play. It was a hard blow at the time ; but he wisely turned to other and better work, and found out, as he grew older, that it would have been the worst thing in the world for him if his crude, boyish writing had received praise it did not deserve.

In 1835, he was thirty-one years of age. By

that **time he had** gained wisdom from books
and travel, and after so many years had passed
he found he had again something **to say** which
must be written for men **to** read.   But this
time it was no play to amuse the pleasure-
seekers **in a** London theatre.   There were
great evils to be mended in the world about
him, and he thought he saw some of the
changes for the better which must be made.
Within twelve months, **he wrote and published**
two **pamphlets.   One of them** he **called** " England, Ireland, and America,**" and the other he
called " Russia."   **This time** he **had** no thought
of gaining fame **by** his **writings.**   On their title-
pages, **the** pamphlets were said to be written by
a Manchester manufacturer ; but no one knew
that Richard Cobden, the hard-working young
calico-printer, was their author.

The fame of these pamphlets spread quickly
through the town.   New editions came out, and
they were read and talked about far beyond the
limits of Manchester.   **Boys** heard their fathers
speak of these striking **writings by** an unknown
author, and they, too, wanted to know who the
hidden person really was whom every one was
so anxious to discover.   What was it Richard

Cobden had said that roused so much inquiry in those days? Before this question can be answered, there is something else to be told.

Three years had gone by since the passing of that Reform Bill in 1832 which the English people had striven so hard to gain. One result of that struggle was that men were wide awake and longing earnestly on all sides for further reforms. There was an active zeal abroad which only needed leading to the right sort of work. With this belief, a large-hearted Scotch lawyer, named George Combe, who had long wished in some way to lessen the sorrows of his fellow-men, had written a book entitled "The Constitution of Man."

In this book, he pointed out the way in which he thought men's lives might be made happier and better. Very soon his book became famous, and was widely read. Richard Cobden met with it, and it seemed to him that thoughts which had lain unnoticed in his own mind hitherto, rose up as answering echoes to the words he read. Perhaps there may be nothing new to us in these later days in teachings that were fresh then. Told in very few words, they were as follows :—

There are certain laws of nature which men are meant to obey, and those people are most happy and wise who find out those laws and follow their commands. By doing so, men learn how to keep healthy bodies and pure, wholesome dwellings. If people would have wise minds and pure souls, they MUST have these healthy bodies and wholesome, pure abodes.

This book came as a welcome gospel to people who wanted to know how to mend the wickedness of the world, and did not know where to begin. What a grand thought it was that in doing good to the *bodies* of men, one touched at the same time the spirit within : that in cleansing a dirty street, or letting sun and air into a dark, close school, one helped to make future angels. Hitherto, people had quite divided soul from body, the inner from the outer life. The " Constitution of Man " told how closely the one acted on the other.

Now Richard Cobden read this book, and he carried the teachings of George Combe still further. As he went about his daily work, he began to see a grand meaning in his cotton-printing, and in all the business to which his life was given up. He believed that a perfect society might be established on earth, and that the great tie of commerce was to be one means of binding men together in honest, kindly, neighbour-loving lives. But to that end, England must change her policy. She must cease to meddle in the quarrels of other nations. She must give up her great standing army, and set the example of a mighty nation walking in the paths of justice and free trade. Commerce and peace might bind the world together. Factories, mills, and furnaces, by spreading prosperity and refinement abroad, would bring about a higher social order; and men, busy in the common ways of trade, might in their own sphere be heralds of peace and unity, and builders of a new and glorious kingdom on earth.

It is a grand thing to have a high motive for the work of life. A tradesman in a little village shop, if he once felt the truth of those ideas that Richard Cobden taught in his pamphlets, might feel his money-making glorified into grand work for humanity.

In the north of England, busy towns were springing up, and busy men were ready to hear any new views concerning commerce. Perhaps some of the readers of Richard Cobden's pamph-

lets began to see that peace **and** goodwill
might follow in the steps of free trade among
nations, if jealous, angry governments would
cease to interfere.   Richard Cobden **saw, how-**
ever, that there were false ideas of honour and
glory abroad.   Yet he hoped better views might
arise among the children who were growing up
to fill their fathers' places.   So he tried to estab-
lish new schools ; and whenever he was invited,
he spoke at meetings **in** support **of** education,
and did all in his power, like a good **knight, to**
fight against ignorance in the world about him.

One morning, as he **sat** writing **in his** office
in Manchester, a stranger from **Rochdale was**
shown **in who** wished **to** speak with him.
Richard Cobden looked up from his desk, **and**
saw a young man with open, earnest face, **whose**
straightforward words and manner made **him**
welcome at once.   The stranger's **errand** was
soon told.   It **was** to **ask Mr.** Cobden to speak
at a meeting **on** behalf **of** education, which he
had called in Rochdale **for an** early evening.
Richard Cobden's **face** lighted **up** with sym-
pathy.   He agreed to the request at once, and
that morning the great friendship between the
two young men began which lasted all their lives.

CHAPTER VII.

"GREEN BANK."

ALL dwellers in Rochdale knew the large old-fashioned family house called "Green Bank," which stood in the middle of the town. There lived the good Quaker, Jacob Bright, with his large family. He had built the dwelling years before when a young man, and his children had grown up in it. Jacob Bright was a cotton-spinner, as his father had been before him, and his mill stood in Rochdale. Numbers of the townspeople had worked there all their lives, and had found a good master in Jacob Bright. Of one thing every one felt sure, that the promise of the good old Quaker gentleman was always to be trusted, and that honour and integrity were to be found in him at all times. So a good atmosphere hung over Green Bank

and its old-fashioned, shady garden, lying like a
forgotten country nook in the midst of the little
town ; and worthy influence spread from it into
the narrow streets and work-places beyond its
walls.

It was the eldest son of this family, named
John Bright, who came as a stranger to the
counting-house in Manchester, with his request
for help. No wonder that Richard Cobden,
though seven years his senior, felt drawn at
once to the young cotton-spinner who stood
before him. Richard had learned to look
below the surface for what was real in character,
and grand and true influences had acted on
John Bright from his birth, and he had grown
worthy of them all.

In early boyhood he had listened to stories
about his faithful Quaker forefathers, who had
gladly suffered persecution and even death
rather than fail at all in truth and duty.
Mingled with the memory of these stories came
that of his dead mother who had told them to
him ; and they became in later youth sacred
examples in the spirit of which he must walk.
His training had been careful and thorough in
the country school where some of his early life

JOHN BRIGHT.

had been spent. He had learned from the study of past history to enter into that new history which his own country was making for herself day by day, and to throw his heart into the troubles and victories of his own time. Plain-spoken, true, and honest was young John Bright. Much study of the grand old Bible words had made his language clear and to the point, and he had a power of eloquence always ready to break forth at need. He was a lover of poetry, too, and read it. Thanks to this taste, visions of beauty often came to the soul of this youth, whose outer life lay to so great an extent among noisy wheels and rough mill work. Though full of energy and strong of will, he had so tender a heart that the sorrows of the men and women about him touched him sometimes to tears.

Such was the character of Richard Cobden's visitor. Both the young men were in earnest, and had high aims. So it was no wonder that a friendship sprang up between them. Richard Cobden went to the meeting in Rochdale, and that night slept under the roof of the Quaker's peaceful home.

Every month some new interest arose in

Cobden's busy life. To his friends it must have seemed strange to look back to those far-off days when he had been only a little shepherd-lad on the Sussex downs. Yet all seemed natural to him. Probably he never asked himself the secret of the progress he had made. Had he done so, he might have found it in his boyish determination to make good use of all the little chances sent him, and in the upward and onward aim from which he had never afterwards turned aside.

About this time, he carried out some new business plans, and took an active part in public affairs in Manchester. He was made an alderman. Men who wanted advice or help thought at once of young Richard Cobden, and he was ready for them all. But so many interests brought a great strain upon him, and in 1836, the year when his pamphlets came out, he was advised to go abroad again in search of rest and change. His partners, somewhat anxious about his health, gladly set him free. Then letters from him were eagerly looked for by his family. They came often, and were so full of clear accounts of all he saw and heard, that, as his sisters read them, the town house, and even the dull Manchester street in which they lived, seemed to brighten with a fresh, new life.

As usual, Richard was gaining wisdom and experience by travelling. He was looking behind the scenes, and learning lessons from foreign trade and government, so that he might know how to help his own country-men if ever he had the power to do so.

One day, unexpected news came to him from England. He learned that a plan was on foot to send him to Parliament at the next General Election. He was to be proposed as member for Stockport, which was one of the Lancashire towns to which the Reform Bill of 1832 had given the new right of representation.

" Don't spoil your holiday by being anxious over this matter," wrote one of his friends. No doubt this man wondered greatly when he read Richard's answer to his advice :—

" I am not giving one moment's thought to the Stockport election. The worthy folks may do as they please. They may make me M.P. by their favour, but they cannot mar my happiness if they reject me. I shall be quite happy whichever way it goes. My peace and

G

happiness do **not depend on** external circumstances of this **or any** similar **nature."**

The fact was, Richard **Cobden's wise** plan was to leave the **future to** unfold itself. He lived in the present. The **time** to work for his election had not yet come, and he must give his mind to the business that lay **at** his hand.

A great event took place in England in the summer **of** 1837. Richard **had been at home** again just two **months when news of** the old king's death spread **through the land.** It was a wonderful **day in London, when** the young Princess Victoria was crowned Queen in Westminster **Abbey. Seldom had such** grand doings **been** known. Foreign princes and envoys **in** their brilliant dresses, and **gay** banners and festoons, shed colour everywhere. A grand public procession passed through the streets of the city, and the cheers **of** the loyal people echoed from **every** house-top and crowded road-way **on the line of** march. Hosts of people from the **country** had flocked in to see the sights ; but behind **all** this excitement lay another **and** a deeper feeling. A great hope had spread among **the** people that with this new reign fresh reforms might arise to lessen the sorrows of the poor.

With the new reign came the need for a new election, and towns large and small were busy and full of life. In Stockport, reformers chose Richard Cobden as their candidate ; but Tories had also their word to say, and a contest arose. Meanwhile, Frederick Cobden, whose character was no less timid and wanting in energy than it had been of old, trembled and had trembled ever since he first heard of this new plan. The business would suffer—of that he was sure—and all would go wrong. His brother was undertaking more than he could do. Such were some of the fears he felt.

Richard, on the contrary, saw a new channel of work opening out before him. All his life he had grieved over the troubles of the people. Who more gladly than he would take up their message to Parliament and try to help them there ? To his brother's fears he made reply that the great business in which he had worked so hard was meant to be a *means* and not an *end*. He wished when death came to be able to think that he had not wasted his life with only heaping up money, but had given part of it to worthier work. Then he threw himself into the struggle, and heartily longed for his election as a means to help him in the work he had to do.

Friends were eager, meetings were numerous, great zeal was shown ; but Richard Cobden was a stranger to the borough, and he failed to win the seat. Lovers of reform in Stockport had heavy hearts when the result of the poll was known. What of their hero who had lost the fight ? *He* had lost neither hope nor courage. Other ways of work lay open to him. Perhaps even this failure might be for the best. Seventeen hundred Liberal working men subscribed one penny each to present him with a piece of plate in token of their respect. A great open-air meeting was held in Stockport, and Richard Cobden addressed the crowd. As the young man looked down upon the sea of eager, upturned faces that met his gaze, he felt within himself the call to be the people's helper, and knew that his time would still come.

CHAPTER VIII.

THE ANTI-CORN-LAW ·LEAGUE.

FAR away across the great North Sea there lies a country rich with many legends and wild tales of olden time. Castles that have stood there for centuries now lie in grand old ruins on the hills, below which broad rivers flow. ·In those old days, however, bands of warriors made these fortresses their stronghold, and went forth armed to the teeth against each other, while the dwellers in the plain beneath took part in the conflicts thus begun. Those were hard days to live in. The peasant found it little worth their while to till the land, for at harvest time the golden crops were never safe from roving enemies. Miners and woodcutters might toil hard in hills and forests, but trade was hopeless in those warlike times, when every river **raft that** bore their **wealth for sale** was **at** the mercy **of** the robber-chiefs, **beneath whose** towers it floated down the Elbe or **Rhine.**

There is a saying, " Time works **wonders."** As the years passed **by, a** wiser generation grew up **in** that unruly land. The various States began **to** learn what they could gain from each other by peaceful interchange—the treasure of the mountains for the forest timber of the neighbouring valley, and the wheat **of** the sunny meadow-land for the cattle **from** the pasture on **the** hills. The dreaded warriors passed out **of** the land **by** degrees, and the ruins of their castles told **the** tale of what had been. This **is no** fairy **story.** It is the true tale of what happened in **a** large part of Germany; and, in the year 1833, the grand news had come to England that the once hostile people had bound themselves together in one great union. Each State had **leave to** grow and manufacture what it chose, and buy and sell with **all** the rest. A treaty **of** Free Trade was made among them. If **such a treaty** could be extended to the **whole** earth, Richard Cobden's happiest dream would be fulfilled.

So thought he in England **in** the year 1837,

when the excitements of the General Election
were over, and autumn came, and the harvest
was gathered in. For that year there was a
failure in English crops ; a bitter winter
followed the bad harvest, and there was great
and widespread distress. Yet in other lands
food was plentiful. There were rich harvests
in countries where many of our manufactured
goods would have been welcome in exchange.
But the cruel Corn and Provision Laws placed
heavy duties on all food imported from abroad.
That winter there were starving thousands
in the sad towns of Lancashire. Of these,
great numbers made their want known by
fierce complaints ; but Richard Cobden knew
of broken-spirited men and lonely, helpless
women who shrunk from public pity, and would
rather die than make their troubles known.

Was it any wonder that one thought seemed
now to fill his eager mind ; that he spoke of
it wherever he went, and that this thought
concerned the great misery which he knew
free trade would remove ? This young trader,
self-made, son of a poor farmer, had, by slow
but sure degrees, made his way to a great
vocation. His mind was set upon as noble a

mission as any preacher **or** reformer placed
before himself **in** the days of old. His aim
was to help the daily life of his **fellow-men,** and
ease their woes. By some means they *must*
have cheap food.

One night he was walking with a friend
through the streets of Liverpool on his way to
a great banquet. As usual, his talk was of the
starving thousands, homeless **and** out of work.
Suddenly **he stood still, and spoke** thus : " **I'll
tell you what we'll do. We'll use the Man-**
chester Chamber **of Commerce for an agitation.
I am** determined **to put** forth **all my strength
for** the repeal of **those** Corn and Provision
Laws."

This was no passing fancy—forgotten when
the banquet was over. The friend to whom
he had spoken knew him for a resolute man.
Soon the English nation would know him too !

The first question was—how should he go
to work ? A man must have wisdom and
experience who would **try to** change the laws
of a nation. Were there **no** lessons to be
learned in those lands through which the
Rhine and Elbe flowed, where free trade had
taken the place of robbery and war ? He

would have a month's holiday, and wander there.

So Richard Cobden carried out this plan, and saw for himself the working of that great commerical treaty. In this visit he learned, too, that men must help themselves, and not trust only to their rulers; that happiness depends on morals and manners more than on politics. He thought of the crowded public-houses at home, and the low pleasures the city people loved, and longed to send a message to the men of wealth and power in England, *to be* noble, and keep a grand ideal before them for their guide.

Richard Cobden was not the first man who had raised his voice against the English Corn Laws. At various times, men had risen in Parliament to protest, and a small society in London had been also formed to urge their repeal. But all the Lords, and far the greater number of the Commons were wealthy land-owners, and would not see the evil that the Corn Laws wrought. A far stronger protest must make itself heard. Where could it rise so well as in Manchester, in the heart of all the trouble?

In October, 1838, a little band of resolute
men—only seven of them—met together there
and formed a new Anti-Corn-**Law** Associa-
tion.   Afterwards, committee meetings **were**
held twice **a** day in **a** dark, little, draughty
room **in** Market Street.   The yearly sub-
scription for every member was five shillings
—a small beginning in every way.   But what
cannot earnestness achieve ?   Richard Cobden
joined the band, and there was **no** harder
worker than he.   He saw the mighty harves**t**
which must grow **out of** that tiny **seed** before
the sower's task was **done; and** first of **all** he
tried to con**vert** his own townsmen **to** the **cause.**

Wonderfully persuasive were his words ; **and**
so clear **were** his arguments, that as people
listened **to** his public speeches, or his private
talk, their doubts and opposition died away.
" Was it not plain," he said, **"that** foreign
countries would not buy our goods unless we
bought freely from them in return **?**   Was it
not plain that while people increased in number
in our towns so fast, we **must** find fresh markets for the goods we made ? otherwise wages
could not be kept up, and our working-men
must starve.   Was it not plain that we were

encouraging competition against us in other lands by obliging them to manufacture goods for themselves, instead of changing with us for their surplus food ? "

Richard Cobden knew well that different motives would act on different minds. Some hard-headed business men could only be led to work against the Corn Laws by arguments such as these. But his own enthusiasm sprang from a better source. To him it was a question of right or wrong; and he believed that a religious spirit should possess the workers for free trade, and with that spirit moving them, their labours could not be in vain.

So his zeal made itself felt; his enthusiasm spread, and warmed the hearts of other men. When the Manchester Chamber of Commerce would have been content with half measures, and with proposing to Government a *less* duty upon corn, Richard Cobden stood firmly for the *whole* right, and cried, "The Corn Laws must be done away; we must have free trade for England!" At a great meeting in Manchester, he proposed a scheme for rousing fresh free trade workers in other towns in England, and binding them altogether in one great union. This plan was carried out, and the Anti-Corn-Law League arose, which was to move the world.

Widespread activity followed the new-born zeal. Anti-Corn-Law tracts were printed, and shed broadcast through the land. Lecturers were sent forth to preach the gospel of Free Trade in all parts. For such expenses money was needed. Daily, great sums from wealthy men poured into the office of the League. Yet, hopeful as all this seemed, the work was only just begun. There were two great parties in England, for the interests of landowners and farmers seemed opposed to those of manufacturers and men in trade. Above all, the Houses of Parliament stood strong in their old rights and traditions. Richard Cobden and the little free trade army would have some fierce battles to fight.

Early in the year 1839 they made their first attack. Petitions for the repeal of the Corn Laws had been drawn up by Mr. Cobden, and signed by half a million of people. These were presented in the House of Commons, and there could no longer be a doubt that "protection" had some resolute enemies in the land. Richard Cobden, from Manchester, and some other delegates from other towns, went up to London to await the end of the debate which followed the presentation of the petitions.

From their hotel across Palace Yard they could see the lighted windows of the House of Commons, in which the debate went on. It lasted five nights. A friendly nobleman visited the anxious delegates as they waited for the end, and he talked to them of their hopes. "You will as soon overthrow the monarchy as the Corn Laws," was his answer to the tale they told.

At last the debate was over, and the votes were taken. There were only 197 votes in favour of repeal, and 342 against it. There stood the fortress still unshaken, and the delegates gloomily made ready to depart. But there was one among them who still said to himself, "All difficulties shall yield to energy." Richard Cobden's faith and courage did not fail him. He reminded his companions of the great reforms which time and energy had wrought in the past. They felt the influence of his brave words, and went home ready to fight new battles for the cause they held so dear.

CHAPTER IX.

STORMING THE FORTRESS.

RICHARD COBDEN and his partners had prospered in trade far beyond any hope they had when, as young men, in the year 1828, they had come to Manchester seeking their fortune. By this time they had four firms, and their printed calicoes were in great demand. Good prospects were before them. They had no longer any need to fear for the future. Yet Richard Cobden was not contented, and for this reason—his love for his brother Frederick was no less strong than it had been in his earlier years. Perhaps with his love was mingled a sort of tender pity for the elder brother, who was less fitted than himself to struggle with difficulties. He could not enjoy any prosperity which Frederick did not share,

The time had come when Frederick must be made a partner in the business which Richard had done so much to form ; and the prospects of the two younger brothers must also be kept in view. But to this new scheme the partners would not agree. Therefore, for his brother's sake, Richard Cobden gave up the hope of ease which lay before him, parted from his old comrades, and began business with Frederick for a partner. This change obliged him to find new capital and a new staff.

At first, all went well. It seemed as if any business must prosper to which Richard Cobden gave his attention. Next year, all his brothers and sisters being well cared for, he married a Welsh lady, who had been long known to the family. One and all were glad that this new joy should come into their faithful brother's life.

But no fresh happiness could turn him even a hair's-breadth from the work he had once felt called to do. Nor could the new cares of his business make him forget the sorrows of the people, which he was resolved to lessen. He was still one of the hardest workers in the Free Trade League.

In those days great spaces of waste land lay in and around the town of Manchester. Mr. Cobden had bought some of this land in the hope that in course of time free trade would so increase the prosperity of England that these open spaces would be worth much for the sites of factories and houses. A sad story belonged to one of the fields he owned. In that field, when Richard was yet a boy in his wretched Yorkshire school, a great gathering of people had met to discuss the new Corn Law. Suddenly, soldiers had broken in upon the peaceful, helpless crowd, and men and women who could not escape in time had been shot or trodden down. Ever since then a terrible memory had clung to that barren field, and people still shuddered when they spoke of the "Massacre of Peterloo."

" I will give a better use to the land," thought Richard Cobden, and one day a hundred workmen were to be seen busily at work upon the ground. In eleven days they had raised a huge wooden building on " Peterloo," and it was known throughout Manchester that Mr. Cobden had given this land for the uses of the League. The great building was the first

" Free Trade Hall." There all the meetings and banquets of the League in Manchester were to be held.

After that the good work went on faster than before. Richard Cobden had no lack of earnest fellow-workers, whose names, with his, will be remembered for years to come. Great gatherings were held in the Hall, with Mr. George Wilson, President of the League, in the chair. Reports of the speeches were printed and sent forth far and wide. What matter that the lecturers who travelled over England met with threats and ill-treatment! They were in earnest, and ignorance and enmity *must* give way before them in the end. What matter that the public papers abused the free-traders, and tried to hinder their work? By that time the penny post had been set on foot, and copies of the free trade papers and tracts made their way into every village in the land, and told a different tale.

Truly England was wakening to new life. A great battle was being fought in her midst, and the two war-cries were " Protection " and " Free Trade."

In 1841, another General Election took place,

with a change in the ministry. The Conservatives came that year into power, and Sir Robert Peel was Prime Minister. Then **those** who loved the Corn Laws rejoiced ; **for was not** Sir Robert Peel a great landowner, and likely **to** protect the farmers of England from the inroads **of** foreign-grown food ?

Before this election, Richard Cobden was again proposed **as** member **for** Stockport. This time, however, **it** was against his will, and he offered £100 towards **the expenses of another** candidate. **For his new** business required constant care, **and he** was **no** longer free to throw himself with an easy mind into public work. But **the** band **of** free-traders in Lancashire could **not do** without **so** great a leader. There **was** only *one* opinion among them—his voice must be heard **in** Parliament against the Corn Laws, **or the** great cause **for** which they were striving would fail. Freedom from close attendance at the House was offered **him.** As he pondered, his path grew plain. No private cares ought **to** keep him **back** from the work Providence was **calling** him **to do.** He was elected for Stockport—a new messenger from the starving people to Parliament—a brave

knight sent forth to storm the strong fortress.

At the opening of the session he took his
seat in the House of Commons, and a few
evenings afterwards he rose to make his
maiden speech. The sight of the young
calico-printer, who dared thus to bring his un-
welcome doctrines to that august assembly,
roused the anger of the great landowners
around him, whose ancestors had sat for
generations in the House. There was little
courtesy shown him. Jeering speeches reached
his ears. It was thought that he would break
down and sink with shame into his seat.

" There's nothing in him—he's only a barker,"
said a man in the Strangers' Gallery, where John
Bright also sat, listening for the first sound of
his friend's voice.

It was no small ordeal to uphold a hated
cause in the stronghold of its enemies ; but a
sense of duty can strengthen a man to any
extent, and Richard Cobden did not care a
rush at that moment for the opinion of the
House. He thought only of his mission. In
clear and simple words he brought forward his
arguments against the Corn Laws. There was

a tone of reality about his **speech** which startled
his hearers **and silenced those** who jeered.
From arguments **he went to facts, and** told **of**
the widespread troubles **of the** people **in** sad
words that touched the **hearts** of many **of his**
hearers.   **In after** years John Bright told the
story of that night, and **said : "** I **could** see the
truth spreading from **his lips and** entering the
minds **of** all **who** heard **him,** till **y**ou could see
in their faces **and eyes that they had** got hold
of a new truth **that they would keep for ever."**

Before his speech was ended, **the new mem-**
ber's pathos changed **to** bold **rebuke.   No**
longer must **the Parliament of** England **talk**
of the interests of **a class** when the **whole**
nation **was** praying for **relief.**   " The day will
come," he cried, " when the people who reverence sacred things will **win** the cause of free
trade, and you and yours will vanish like chaff
before the whirlwind."

So ended Richard Cobden's first speech **in**
the House.   There was no longer any doubt
that **the** new member for Stockport was **in**
deadly earnest, and **would let no man** silence
him.

Well was **it** that the Reform Bill of 1832

RICHARD COBDEN.

had given the right of representation to the people of our northern towns, if by that measure a man like Richard Cobden could find his way into the House of Commons. But he greatly needed support, and often his thoughts turned to his old friend, John Bright, who was working as hard as ever outside the House in many a worthy cause.

Many years had passed since the young Rochdale cotton-spinner's visit to the counting-house of Richard Cobden. The friendship then formed between the two young men had grown closer as years went by. Now, in the autumn of 1841, news came of a heavy sorrow that had fallen on John Bright's newly-made home, and Richard Cobden turned from his pressing public work with a troubled heart to comfort his friend. He set out at once from London to the darkened house at Leamington, where the young wife lay dead, and the broken-hearted husband mourned for her. With the freedom of an old friend he entered. There are sacred moments in human lives of which no one can tell the tale ; but the world knows that Richard Cobden's true heart found a way of giving hope and courage to his friend, and that his words, like heavenly messengers, called back a noble **worker out** of his despair.

" There are thousands of homes **in** England at this moment," he said **at** last, "**where** wives and mothers and children are dying of hunger. Now when the first bitterness of your grief is past, come with me, and we **will** never rest till the Corn Law is repealed."

So they went together, and visited famine-stricken homes, **and saw** afresh the **misery in** large towns. **A great strength was added in** John Bright to **the free trade** cause, **and from** that day Richard **Cobden knew that it must be** won.

The new Premier, **Sir** Robert **Peel,** had stormy prospects before him when **he** took office. Within **a** week after **the** opening **of** Parliament, 994 petitions for the repeal of the Corn Laws had been presented ; and as the members drove along the streets of London to **the** House, they **were** greeted with loud cries demanding the repeal of **the** bread tax.

On **the** other hand, the supporters of the Corn Law **trusted to** the new Premier to uphold the tax, and they watched eagerly for the new budget. When **it** came out, **the** bread tax was still retained. What wonder that the new member for Stockport was in deadly earnest when he had spoken for the first time in the House of Commons?

That year, 1841, the harvest was bad, and there was no work to be had for hosts of starving men. "Protection" had not found a market for English goods. Never was there greater need for men with brave hearts and plain speech, who feared nothing but wrong-doing. Mr. Villiers brought forward in the House his annual motion for the repeal of the Corn Law—in vain. Richard Cobden made speech after speech, always clear and to the point. Grave warnings they were that he gave. He told how English workmen were leaving our shores to find work and food in the New World; how the poor in our own land were eating nettles or starving in idleness, when a wise Government might find food and work for all. They were homely illustrations that he used sometimes; but a high motive filled him with zeal, and made him so eloquent that men held their breath to listen. Yet in return he met with sneers and taunts from those who did not agree with him. His great

hopes were scorned.   He was accused of mean
and selfish motives.   His words were twisted,
and false meanings put upon **them.**   The
Prime Minister, on one occasion, **had an angry**
dispute with him.   After that, it was said that
the ruin of the bold young member was certain,
and the public press declared that at all costs
this disturber of the peace must be destroyed,
and a new law passed against the seditious
body of which he **was** the leader.

Behind all he had private **cares** and anxieties
which were very **heavy to** bear.   Letters came
frequently from his **brother, Frederick** Cobden,
in Manchester, where **his** business was doing
badly and greatly needed his presence.   Truly
he must be **a** brave man who could stand firm
to such **a** post as Richard Cobden held through
such trials.   The fact was, that **such** a religious
spirit as gave strength to reformers and martyrs
of old, possessed this modern young cotton-
printer, and **it** left no room for doubt and
cowardice.   Still the **great** fortress was un-
taken, though the Leaguers **fought** bravely
without and within.

CHAPTER X.

THE VICTORY WON.

THE quiet old city of Durham woke up to new life one summer day in 1843. The narrow streets were gay with flags, and noisy with the steps and voices of busy, hurrying men. All the misery and forced idleness in the town were forgotten for a time, though looms had been long idle, and men, women, and children were suffering hardships because there was no work to do, and bread was so dear. Bursts of music were borne upon the breeze, and echoed round the solemn cathedral tower and venerable castle walls. The sun shone on the distant hills, and sparkled on the water of the river Wear, till it seemed as if a good time might be at hand again for the old town. And truly a better day was near; for John Bright

had been returned member for Durham, and
his large, tender heart was alive to the sorrows
of the people, and the aim of his life, like that
of Richard Cobden, was to be the repeal of the
Corn Laws.

It was not only in the House of Commons
that the voices of the two friends were raised.
There were times when debates on other
matters went on there, and set them free; and
there were seasons, too, when tired members
rested from their labours, on the moors or by
the sea-side. But, on such occasions, there
was no rest for Richard Cobden and John
Bright. In sultry sunshine, in storm and
rain, they travelled over England and Scotland,
holding meetings in country places, to teach
the ignorant people the blessings free trade
might bring. Richard Cobden had no love for
public meetings. He often said it would be a
great relief to him if he knew he had never to
make another speech. Moreover, the claims
of home life and his private business were
pressing heavily on him every hour. So, great
self-denial was needed in leading his hard-
worked public life.

In their journeys they met with strange

experiences. They were greeted with abusive
words ; even brickbats and stones were hurled
at them. But by degrees they gained an
influence over the people. Open-air meetings,
which they called together, were crowded.
Farmers, fearing the anger of their landlords
at home, travelled, in some cases, thirty or forty
miles to places where they were not known, that
they might listen in safety to the great speakers
on this wonderful scheme of free trade in corn.
Strong feeling moved the listeners when
Richard Cobden told them how he himself
had once been a country lad, and kept his
father's sheep, and had known the misery of
rent-day. As they listened to the stirring words
of the orators, their dull faces cleared, and
their eager hands were held up to vote for the
repeal of the Corn Law. Sometimes starving
labourers, anxious to help in their own poor
way, would come up to ask where the fighting
was to be. It was a labour of time to teach
such men what peaceful workers could do by
influence and speech alone ; but, by degrees,
a better hope than that of wild revenge grew
up in these troubled hearts, and they learned
to trust the heroes who were working for

them, and to know that God had raised them up.

So it came to pass, at last, that when their names were uttered at a public meeting, the people with one accord would rise and give hearty cheers for the brave men who were giving up time and strength in the effort to untax the people's bread.

It would take too long in this short story of Richard Cobden's life to tell of all the mighty deeds done by the members of the Anti-Corn-Law League. Rich men, who knew how much of their success in life depended on the opening of foreign markets, gave large sums of money willingly. Huge meetings were held in the great Covent Garden Theatre, in London ; and both there and in Manchester, grand bazaars were opened, where countless men and women, whose names are not recorded, used all their powers to help to win the struggle. It is strange to look back from those times to the early days when seven earnest-hearted men began the work in a small gloomy room in Manchester, and when Richard Cobden stopped his friend in the streets of Liverpool, to say : " I will from this time put forth all my strength for the repeal of the Corn and Provision Laws."

The autumn of 1845 set in wet and cheerless. The fields were soaked with steadily falling rain, and terrible tidings came over from Ireland. There the potato crop had failed; the food in which the people trusted was not to be had, and the harvest in England had failed. Famine and disease were spreading among the Irish people, and the cry was raised more loudly than ever: "Open the ports! untax the people's bread!" In these gloomy days, Richard Cobden was called to Manchester by bad news, and a friend calling on him in his counting-house, found him one afternoon, in the deepening twilight, utterly cast down. Ruin threatened his business, and he could see no other course open to him than that of retiring at once from public life.

He told this resolution in a letter to his friend John Bright, who was then staying at Aberdeen, in the north of Scotland. It was a hard step to take, for the great battle he had been fighting so long was nearly won, and his friend knew how heavy must be the trouble to one whose heart was in the cause. Moreover, the loss of Richard Cobden's help would be a great loss to the free-traders : it might even be the ruin of their plans. In reply, a letter came from Aberdeen, which cheered the heart of the despairing man, and he began once again to believe in his old motto, " All difficulties shall yield to energy."

Through storm and rain John Bright followed his letter. Long and weary the journey seemed, and slow the pace of the post-horses that carried him through the dreary, misty country to his friend. But when he reached Manchester, he did not rest till he had found means to settle the business troubles of Mr. Cobden's firm ; and its Principal was once more able, though not without a heavy weight of care, to work for the Anti-Corn-Law League.

It was quite true that, in that gloomy autumn of 1845, the end of the great struggle was at hand. Multitudes of men, women, and children in the kingdom were dying daily of famine and disease, and in some way every one agreed that food must be found for them if their misery was to end. But party-strife ran high. Both Whigs and Tories had many schemes to propose ; only the Leaguers were of one mind.

Richard Cobden's health failed. Still, he took no rest. If any lesser motive than the love of duty had influenced him, he must now have broken down; but that was the mainspring of all his energy, and it would not let him fail. So he continued to summon public meetings, and to address them, and lost no chance of upholding free trade counsels in the House.

Could it be that Sir Robert Peel, the friend of the Corn Laws, was beginning to waver? Richard Cobden thought he saw signs of this, and took fresh courage.

Early in the year 1846, the Queen opened Parliament in person. There were rumours abroad of a great surprise at hand. Sir Robert Peel had given notice that in a few nights he should bring forward the subject of the Corn Laws for discussion in the House of Commons. At the appointed time, the Strangers' Gallery was crowded. No such excitement had been known since the year 1832, when the Reform Bill was passed. Within the last few days a letter by Lord John Russell had been published. In this letter he had openly declared himself in favour of free trade in corn. Lord John Russell was leader of the opposition, and there

I

had been some whispers **of** disagreement in the Cabinet, and of a new Liberal Government. Still, however, **Sir** Robert Peel **was Prime** Minister. What course would **he** pursue? There was a great silence through the House when he rose **to** speak, and very soon it was plain to the listening crowd that his opinions had changed, and that he was now willing to repeal the Corn Law.

A man becomes **a hero when** he listens **to** the voice **of** conscience, **and** upholds **what he** believes **to be right and** just, **although** expediency and **personal comfort tempt him to** keep silence. It was **the** grandest hour of Sir Robert Peel's life. **To** acknowledge that he had **been in the** wrong **for** so long **was** a painful task. He knew that by doing **so** he would call down upon himself the fierce reproaches of his **own** party; that his followers would accuse him of treachery to their cause, and would desert him. But he had never yet used his power for any unworthy purpose, and **in** this great hour of temptation **he** could be true and brave. **He had to pay a** heavy price for his courage afterwards, in the loss of old friends and **of** office; but the Corn Law

Repeal Bill was carried by a large majority, and afterwards passed the House of Lords : and another record stood for ever of a man who could hold firmly to the right, rather than to that which was worldly-wise and safe.

Yet Sir Robert Peel took no credit to himself when the great victory was at last won. As he took his leave of office, he did honour to the brave man who had been as a thorn in his side for so long, in these words : " The name which ought to be and will be associated with the success of these measures is the name of a man who, acting from pure and disinterested motives, has advocated them with untiring energy, and with appeals to reason, enforced by eloquence, the more to be admired because it is so unaffected and unadorned—the name of *Richard Cobden.*"

Thus at last, in 1846, the Corn Law was repealed, and the faithful workers in the cause of free trade saw their long struggle at an end.

In the month of July, 1846, the last great meeting of the League was held in the Manchester Town Hall. It had done its work, and the time had come for the workers to disband and enter upon other tasks. One after another the well-known heroes entered the Hall and took their seats upon the platform. The great building was shaken with the cheers that greeted them. When Richard Cobden, worn in health and ruined in fortune, by the strain and over-work of years, appeared, it is said that strong men, touched by a deep emotion they were unused to feel, bowed their heads to hide their sudden tears.

The President told again the story of the small beginning—how a few earnest men had met together in a Manchester office, how the work had spread, and the brave leaders had given time and strength and influence, and how even famine and disease had proved messengers from heaven, and helped on the mighty work.

When Richard Cobden rose, he had to stand in silence for some minutes before the great assembly, until the cheers ceased which had broken forth afresh and drowned his words. When at length he could be heard, he gave the glory of the victory to his fellow-workers, and spoke of the grand courage of Sir Robert Peel, and the brave toil of the multitudes of men and women, unknown to fame, without whose help the battle could never have been won. He showed his true greatness in that generous, modest speech, and took his farewell of the League with glad words of prophecy that its influence would not end, but spread abroad in other good works, and in a spirit of good-will and peace among men.

CHAPTER XI.

MIDHURST.

THE summer days of 1846 were in their beauty when Richard Cobden went with his wife and family to a quiet Welsh valley, to seek for rest. and for new strength to meet his business troubles again. While there, he learned, in a welcome and unexpected way, that he would still have it in his power to go on working for the good of his fellow-men. Nearly eighty thousand pounds had been subscribed by his friends as a token of their gratitude for his past labours, which had ruined his own prospects. Thankful for this fresh chance given him to serve his nation, he accepted the gift. First of all, private business claims must be met. When this was done, he was free to leave Manchester and his calico-printing, and to seek a new home elsewhere.

Under these circumstances, his thoughts turned to the old farm-house at Midhurst, in Sussex, where he was born, and where his fore-fathers had lived. He bought the place, with its fields and garden, and made a home there, glad to think that his children would grow up amid sweet country sights and sounds ; and, faithful still to Frederick Cobden, he would not part from him. So the elder brother made one of the family in the new home, and ended his days free from care.

By-and-by a new house was built on the site of the old farm. From its windows, and from the terrace-walk below them, there was a view over the neighbouring wooded country. Thus, Richard Cobden came back, towards the end of life, to the scenes he had loved when a boy. But he was a man of action, and could not rest long. Life was passing quickly, and the work he had set himself to do was not yet done. If he had been an ambitious man, his highest hopes might have been satisfied ; for a seat in the Cabinet was offered him, and honours were pressed upon him. All were declined, however, that he might have great freedom in his plans. These were soon formed.

It was not enough for him that the Corn Law was abolished in England. Beyond her borders lay lands in Europe which knew nothing of the blessings of free trade. Richard Cobden was more than an Englishman—he was a lover of his whole race; and thus he wrote to a friend: "With God's help I must, during the next twelve months, visit all the large States of Europe, and try to enforce those truths which have been irresistible at home."

So Richard Cobden said good-bye to his country home and his English friends, and began his wanderings in foreign lands. Wherever he went, he was welcomed heartily. Banquets were held in his honour, and kings and great statesmen gave him audience. He never lost a chance of preaching his doctrine of free trade, hoping, by its means, to extend commerce, and thus bring peace and good-will among nations. Not only so: wherever he saw wrong done, or an evil custom that *could* be mended, he did not hesitate to speak a word in season; and his speech was powerful because his soul was true.

During his absence, a General Election took place in England. He was returned, both for

the borough of Stockport and the great West Riding of Yorkshire, and accepted the latter post. To be chosen by so large a constituency was a high honour, and added to his chances of influence. He came home with his mind filled with many projects, and worked with a will at them all. The rule of his life at this time was to do with all his might whatever he did, and his friends told each other sadly that he could not fail to shorten his days by such constant labour.

Richard Cobden had a great hope before him—to reach it had really been the aim of all his work in life. This hope was, to bring peace on earth and goodwill among men. As he walked on the quiet, sunny terrace at Midhurst one day, he said to a friend, " I could die happy if I had contributed a little to the partial disarmament of the world."

That day, he turned himself afresh to the task. It was a simple matter that he proposed —that all nations should agree to refer disputes to arbitration, and should reduce their military and naval armaments. Such a proposal he brought before Parliament in 1849, but failed to gain a hearing. His next step was to join in summoning Peace Congresses in various towns in Europe, to try, by their means, to unite nations in a league against war.

But in 1852 a panic arose in England. It was said that the French emperor was going to invade our shores. By speeches, and by the writing of pamphlets, Richard Cobden tried to calm the fears and passions of his countrymen. Within a short time the Crimean War was raging, and the Emperor was the faithful ally of the English. Then came a dispute with China—an unjust one in Richard Cobden's view. Through all these changes, he and his friend, John Bright, stood firm to principle, and at all seasons opposed the widespread thirst for war. But almost all England was against them. They lost the favour they had gained as champions of free trade. They were called traitors to their country, and abused on every hand. In the struggle against the Corn Laws, firm friends had given them courage, and the voices of the eager, hungry multitudes in the great northern towns had cheered them on. *Now* they stood almost alone ; yet they were still true to their own convictions.

Richard Cobden lost his seat in Parliament.

There was a General Election in 1857, and to stand again for the West Riding was out of the question with this loss of popular favour. So he offered himself as candidate for Huddersfield, and failed. The election was gained by a supporter of the Crimean War. But the defeated member went down to Midhurst with a clear conscience, and left the result of his words and deeds for the future to unfold.

Few men reap the harvest of the seeds they have sown. The influence of such a man as Richard Cobden is living and working still; but he *did* live to see statesmen gain faith in arbitration as a means of settling the quarrels of nations; and within three years after the repeal of the Corn Law, he knew that 5,000,000 people were living on corn brought from foreign lands.

By the time Richard Cobden was fifty years of age, he had filled those years with more thought and work than most men expend in a much longer life. Yet through that busy lifetime, while he was first making his own way in the world, and afterwards fighting great battles against wrong, he was still gentle and tender, as all great souls always are. So one must not forget, in the story of this hero's public deeds, his boyish love and reverence for the shabby little home with its broken fortunes; his tenderness for the old father; and his faithful care and self-sacrifice for the elder brother, who failed in all he undertook. At last, in 1856, a great grief fell upon this tender heart, and he went down from London to Midhurst to break the sad tidings to his wife, and tell her that their only son, a boy at school in Germany, was dead. Unknown to them, he had been ill of scarlet fever for many days; for the message to the absent parents had been delayed by some mistake.

It was evening when Richard Cobden reached his home. The merry little children were at play, and he could hear their happy voices as his wife met him on the threshold, and read the terrible news in his face. Then followed months of tender, patient care for her, when he gave up all interests for her sake, travelled with her, and nursed her back to health and hope.

In 1859 he was again in Parliament as member for Rochdale, which place he represented till his death. The anger against him for his opposition to war had died away. Probably there was no influence stronger in the House than his; and true and honest men of all opinions had learned, if they could not agree with him, that he was one whom all might trust. He still had great aims and high ideals before him, as in his youth; and still he was firm and true to them as ever. One more of his great deeds must be told before this story ends. In 1860 he brought about a treaty of commerce between England and France.

"Rare is the privilege of any man," said Mr. Gladstone, "who, having fourteen years ago rendered his country one signal service, once more again, within the same brief space of life, decorated neither by land nor title, bearing no mark to distinguish him from the people he loves, has been permitted to perform another great and memorable service to his sovereign and his country."

Truly rare patience and courage were needed in this work, for the hindrances were great, and the opposition to the treaty in both nations was strong and hard to overcome. Twelve months passed away before his task was done. He began it as a private individual, though he was afterwards supported by the State; and as plain Richard Cobden, he sought the Emperor's presence, and laid before him his plans for the bond of union between the two countries. Marvellous did his influence seem as the stories of the frequent interviews between the dreaded emperor and the peace-loving English hero, were taken up and told from land to land. While Cobden was still about his work, there were fresh rumours of war with France, and of new defences to be made against her on the English coast. Had not the emperor learned how thoroughly he could trust to the honour and word of Richard Cobden, he would never have signed the treaty. In November, 1860, this was done, and the new bond between France and England was firm. Then from both grateful nations came fresh offers of title and honour. But all were declined. This English hero was simply Richard Cobden till his death.

After this, though still at times active in the House, and great in his peaceful influence in the foreign affairs of England, his strength failed slowly. His last pamphlet called "The Three Panics" was published in 1862. His last public speech was made at Rochdale in November, 1864. That winter was spent in his happy home at Midhurst, and in the early days of the following spring, he and his old friend John Bright used to walk and talk together on the terrace.

Was it a sudden, heavenly message that came to him one day and told him that his faithful work on earth was nearly done ? One morning as they thus walked together, he pointed to the spire of the village church, and said, " My boy lies over there, and I shall be with him before many days."

It was a true prophecy. Not long after, when the cold March winds were blowing, he travelled to London that he might be present in the House when an important debate went on. But he was seized with bronchitis. For more than a week, his friends watching by his bedside did not lose hope of his recovery. Then a change came, and they knew the end was near. On Sunday morning, April 2nd, 1865, Richard Cobden's spirit was called to higher life, and a few days after they laid his body in the churchyard among the pine trees in the place where he was born.

Was not *he* a hero, who was true from boy-hood to great aims in life, and who bravely did his duty through evil and good report?

So thought the members of the **House of** Commons, his old companions, when they **heard** that **he was** dead.   **The** following day the Prime Minister, amid deep silence, spoke of the **great** loss the country had sustained ; and **John** Bright's broken words found an echo in many hearts when he spoke of " the manliest, **gentlest spirit that ever** quitted a human form."

Butler & Tanner, The Selwood Printing Works, Frome, and London.